The Bent-Back Bridge

The Bent-Back Bridge

Gary Crew

Gregory Rogers

Lothian
BOOKS

Thomas C. Lothian Pty Ltd
11 Munro Street, Port Melbourne, Victoria 3207

This edition published 1995
Reprinted 1995
First published as 'Sleeping Over at Lola's' in
Hair-raising: ten horror stories, Omnibus, Sydney, 1992

National Library of Australia
Cataloguing-in-publication data:

Crew, Gary, 1947– .
  The bent-back bridge.
  ISBN 0 85091 704 2.
  I. Title. (Series: After dark series).
A823.3

Illustration media: charcoal, pastel and ink
Cover design by Dennis Ogden
Printed in Australia by The Griffin Press

The bus rattled across a wooden bridge and turned off the road. Janet looked up from her book. Is this it? she wondered, and cupped her hands against the window to peer into the night. The bus had stopped in a clearing among the roadside scrub, but through the darkness she could make out the yellow glow of a telephone box. There it is, she said to herself, like Lola said.

The driver cut the engine and pushed the cap back from his forehead. 'Here we are,' he called without turning. 'Terminus.'

Janet closed her book and glanced over her shoulder to the rear of the bus. There were no other passengers. She reached for the duffel bag at her feet, then heaved herself out of the seat. As she stood, her book slipped from her lap and fell to the floor with a thud.

The driver had been watching in the mirror. 'You right there, love?' he called.

Janet did not answer. She bent to retrieve the book, then, straightening, made her way up the aisle. She did not look at the driver – though she sensed his eyes on her – and felt herself colouring as the little troll key ring that dangled from her bag clinked noisily against the chromed handrails of the empty seats. When she reached the end of the aisle, she slung the bag over her shoulder, ready to step out.

The driver looked up and grinned. 'I suppose you'd like that opened?' he said, nodding towards the door. Janet managed a faint smile. 'Well ...'

He held his chin and shook his head, pretending to think it over. 'I better do the right thing, but it's a dark old night for a pretty girl like yourself to be out there alone ...' Then, with a suddenness that made her wince, a silver lever shot forward and the door burst open.

Janet stepped out into the night.

It was very dark. All about the clearing the bush was thick and threatening, but there was the phone box, 20 metres away. Janet turned up her collar, hitched the duffel bag at her shoulder and reached into her pocket for the note Lola had written:

> If you come, take the 403 to the Bent-Back Bridge terminus. I'll meet you at the phone box about 10 p.m. That's when I go walking. You'll get to meet Patch too. Sure hope you make it. *Lola.*

Lola was the closest Janet had ever come to having a friend. Generally people ignored her, or were cruel to her, like the bus driver – she knew he was laughing at her when she dropped her book, when she galumphed up the aisle, when he called her pretty.

Janet knew exactly what she looked like – 'Janet the Planet' the girls in her physical education class called her.

But when Lola had turned up at school, things changed.

Lisa Harvey, whose silver-blonde hair fell in wavelets to her waist, had been waiting in Administration to collect a lunch pass when Lola enrolled. Lisa told the class that the new girl did not even arrive with a parent – she had enrolled herself. And when she appeared at the classroom door at the elbow of the headmistress, instead of looking down at her feet and fumbling with her hankie she had stared straight at the class, sizing everyone up.

The rest of the girls hated Lola on sight, but Janet was terrified of her. Lola was a big girl too; not overweight like Janet, but tall and powerfully built, with shoulders as wide as an axe handle. She was not wearing school uniform, but a grubby cotton print dress; in fact, as Lisa Harvey informed the class at recess, it looked suspiciously second-hand. And she smelt: 'Musty,' Lisa Harvey said, flicking her hair. 'Like a dog. Like a stinking wet dog.'

Janet listened from a distance. Oh dear, she thought, I hope she doesn't come near me! I hope she doesn't pick on me!

But she did. The new girl noticed her right away. By the end of the first day, whenever Janet looked up from her work she saw that Lola was watching her. Not staring exactly, as the other girls stared, with a sneer in their eyes; more like admiring. As if she liked her. On the second day, when Janet was caught with the answers to the history quiz written on the inside of her arm and made to stand at the front of the room for punishment, it was Lola who kept looking at her when everyone else went back to their work. This was a look that said, Hey, I'm on your side, and soon Janet held her head up and stopped snivelling.

Within a week Lola was sitting with Janet at every break. She would wander over and say, 'Nobody sitting with you again?' or 'What's for lunch today?' or 'I heard what they were saying

12

about you in history. It's not true that you cheat on every test ... is it?'

Once Lola said, 'When they call you Janet the Planet, just pretend it's because you look like a star ... don't think it's because you're fat.'

Even though Lola was sometimes cruel and hurt her feelings, Janet could not stop thinking of her; what it would be like to be so strong; to be game enough never to wear a uniform; not to care what anyone said about you – even to have a name like Lola. Imagine being called Lola and not Janet. Someone called Lola could be anyone she wanted!

When they were together, Janet always gave Lola some of her morning-tea bun, or lunchtime roll, or after-school ice cream. Lola never seemed to bring anything to eat. But there were compensations. It was Lola who stood up for Janet when she let her team down in the swimming carnival. 'Forget about them,' she said. 'Come on, give me some of your cream bun.' It was Lola who took her side when the Relief for African Orphans contribution box went missing – but Janet felt awkward later when Lola produced a handful of small change at

Nicely's Milk Bar, demanding a triple chocolate malted. She felt worse when Mr Nicely looked from one to the other and asked, 'One straw or two?' and Lola had answered firmly, without consultation, 'One. My friend's on a diet.'

And while she was happy when Lola asked if she could be her partner in the biology experiment, Janet could not watch as her new-found friend dissected their live frog without chloroform.

But at the end of term, when Lola called her down into the scrub at the far end of the school grounds and presented her with a gift, 'Something special,' Lola said, 'a secret,' Janet was thrilled.

'I got it myself,' Lola said. 'Especially for you,' and she placed a tiny package of grubby tissue in Janet's hand. Janet's fingers shook as she opened it. Could it be a pendant? Or a bracelet – a gold bracelet with her name engraved? In her open palm lay a plastic and metal key ring shaped like a troll. 'Oh,' she said, touching its shock of blue-black hair, 'it's ...'

'It's gorgeous!' Lola crowed. 'Just like me!'

'But ...' Janet began, afraid that this had also

14

been paid for from the fund for the African Orphans, 'it must have been expensive.'

Lola looked at her in amazement. 'I never bought it, stupid. I took it. I went into Woolies and pinched it. So it's really special, see? Because of the risk.'

Janet nodded and attached the thing to the zip of the duffel bag that she took to school every day. She wasn't happy, but she did it. She'd never had a friend before, and this seemed a small price to pay to keep one.

Then the invitation to sleep over came – or at least was stuffed in her hand one recess. Janet read it quickly, hardly believing, then took it into the toilets, locked the cubicle and read it again. And again. *I want you to come and visit. You could sleep over. But don't tell the others. Secrets are always best. If you come ...*

No girl had ever asked Janet to her house before, not even to listen to records after school; and now an invitation to sleep over. Like a pyjama party. Sitting up until morning, talking and eating chocolates. Both of them in nighties, like the other girls. Why not? she thought. Her parents were going to her great-aunt and uncle's. Sleeping over at Lola's would be better than tea and scones and all that morbid oldies' talk about hernias and melanomas and who might be the next in the family to 'pass on'.

So she said, 'Thank you, Lola. I would love to sleep over,' and here she was, right on time at the Bent-Back Bridge terminus, lugging her duffel bag with her nightie and favourite tapes and magazines and chocolates and ... but there was no sign of Lola. There was just a phone box in a clearing in the bush.

I'll go to the phone box and wait, she thought. Lola can't be too long. As she folded the note to slip it in her pocket, the engine of the bus roared into life. She glanced back. The door was still open; the driver leaned towards her, tipping his cap. 'I'm off, love. Back at midnight, and that's the last of it. Hope you're not still here then.' The door shut and the bus moved off, bumping and shuddering on to the bitumen. Janet watched it clatter across the timber planking of the bridge, the light from the windows growing smaller and paler as it vanished into the night. Like an ocean liner, she thought. Like the lights of the Titanic.

18

She walked to the phone box and dropped her bag in the rectangle of light that spilled from its door. She stood and waited. No one came, not after five minutes, nor ten. By the time fifteen had passed, she felt uneasy. She was certain that her watch was right. It had said ten o'clock when the bus had dropped her. She took the note from her pocket, unfolded it and read aloud, '... the 403 ... Bent-Back Bridge terminus ... 10 p.m.' She looked again. The time was written right on a fold, and the paper had been handled so often, folded so many times. Was it ten? Or ...? No, she was being stupid. There was no mistake, but – and she turned the note over, holding it to the light to check – there was no phone number anywhere.

For the first time she realised: she couldn't ring Lola even if she wanted to. In all the excitement, she hadn't thought; she had been so certain Lola would be there. Like friends are supposed to be. And if no one came, if she was left alone, she couldn't ring her parents; being her first time away she would never be allowed out again. So, she would wait. Lola would come. Lola had said she would and she would because she was her friend.

Janet shifted her bag to the entrance of the phone booth and sat down, leaning back against the door. But when she was settled and looked up, the ring of bush seemed closer, the night darker. She shuddered.

At ten-thirty she could wait no longer. I'll ring information, she thought. They'll have Lola's number. She got up and opened the door of the booth. She stood on tiptoe to read the weathered print of the directory above the telephone. 'Directory Assistance,' she read aloud, '013.' She raised her right hand to dial and with her left she reached for the earpiece. Nothing. Her left hand grasped air. The earpiece was not in its cradle. She looked down. It dangled loose, its cord reaching almost to the floor. She took hold of it and put it to her ear. No dial tone. She jiggled the cradle. No sound at all. 'What?' she said, disbelieving, and placed the instrument back in its cradle, only to lift it immediately, listening again.

Nothing.

She repeated the process, this time jamming the earpiece down.

She lifted it again.

Nothing.

She replaced it carefully. 'Please,' she whispered. 'Please ...' Then, without causing so much as a click, she lifted it and listened again.

The line was dead.

She let the earpiece fall and brought up her hands to press against her mouth. 'No,' she pleaded. 'Don't let this happen.' She lifted her head, steadying herself, and saw the emergency numbers on the wall in front of her. Nodding and muttering, she reached down and grasped the cord swinging beside her. She replaced the earpiece, then, lifting it again, dialled a number that she read aloud. '000,' she said.

She waited, listening.

Nothing.

She hung up and dialled again. This time she said the number distinctly, her voice very firm, as she dialled, '0 ... 0 ... 0.'

But there was nothing; she was listening to silence.

'It will be all right,' she said to herself. She replaced the earpiece gently and turned to the door. Immediately she was struck by the sight of her own reflection staring at her from the glass. She was caught off guard by the fear in the eyes, the down-turned mouth, the pallor of the skin. She moaned, and opened the door.

A path of light appeared suddenly at her feet, then darkness. She lifted her head, looking across the clearing towards the road. There were no street lights, not out here, and she could make out very little except the darker outline of the trees beyond the clearing. To her right was the silhouette of the bridge, like a beast, she thought, arched like the spine of a feeding beast. Quickly she turned away. To the left the bush seemed denser, the night blacker. She could not make out a road at all. 'No wonder it's the terminus,' she mumbled. 'It's the end of the road.' There did not appear to be a house – not even at a distance.

She crossed the clearing to the edge of the bitumen and looked left and right again. If she went left, the road stopped dead at a wall of bush 20 metres away. She turned right and, walking to the centre of the road, followed the white line until it stopped abruptly where the wooden planking of the bridge began. The domed heads of the great metal bolts that secured the planks glinted silver. She stepped on to the bridge and felt the timbers rattle beneath her. It's those awful nails that pin the planks down, she thought, and stood still, listening to the silence. 'Don't be stupid,' she said aloud. 'You're giving yourself the willies.' She forced a laugh and walked on, the sound of the planks against the nails following her, clink ... clink ... clink.

Where the arch of the bridge peaked, she paused to look about. Where could Lola live? she wondered. There isn't even a building. Then another thought crossed her mind: Unless this is a joke. Unless Lola is playing a joke ... Unless she is out to get me, like all the others. She shook her head to dispel the possibility and looked over the handrail.

Beneath the bridge was a pool of darkness. She could not even guess how far the drop was, or what it fell to – it might fall to a gutter or a bottomless abyss. As she craned her neck, looking down, she shuddered involuntarily and pulled back from the rail to look about. Someone's watching, she thought. But there was nobody, nothing, except for the phone box, its distant light warm and inviting. 'This is ridiculous,' she said, and stamped her foot on the planking so that it shook. 'I'll try the phone again. If it's dead, I'll get the midnight bus home.'

She walked determinedly towards the clearing.

At the phone box she checked the directory for the service difficulty number, and dialled again. Silence. Well then, she thought, if that's the way it is, I'll sit in here and wait. She glanced at her watch. It was almost eleven; an hour to the last bus. 'Yes,' she said, 'that's what I'll do.'

She went out and recovered her duffel bag. Back inside the phone box she slipped to the floor and put the bag on her knee to open it. But when she reached for the troll on the zip, it was gone – only the silver key ring remained. She went outside.

Beyond the light from the phone box she could see nothing and in minutes she was back, digging in the bag for her book. 'I'll come and look for that troll in the morning,' she said, adding, 'if I'm still here.' She glanced up to check the position of the light on the ceiling and leaned forward so that her book was well lit. Then, with a further glance at her reflection and a sigh of resignation, she began to read.

In minutes a bevy of tiny moths was fluttering about her face. Some caught in her hair, some flopped around in circles on the open pages.

'Go away,' she whispered as she brushed them off. 'Go on. Shoo.'

But when a black beetle flew in at the gap below the door, whirred about and beat itself against her face, she was not so gentle; she raised her book and swatted the insect. It struck the glass with a smack and fell to the floor on its back, hissing.

'Serves you right,' she said, but as she settled to read again, she caught a movement other than her own – a furtive, slinking movement – outside the darkened glass. She froze, staring at the panels of glass that showed no more than herself – her knees drawn up, hands gripping the pages in her lap, shoulders hunched, her pale hair flopped forward. But there was something out there, she knew. Something circling the phone box – something that had the wit or instinct to remain beyond her vision, circling at the darker edge of the light that spilled from her haven in the box.

Is it human or animal? she wondered. She dared not cup her hands against the glass to see, nor could she trust her legs to stand so that she could throw open the door and shout, 'Get away! Leave me alone, whatever you are!' So she sat, her eyes wide with terror, her ears tuned to the slightest sound. Then it came. A snuffling first, like someone gasping for air; then softer, a padding sound ... puff ... puff ... puff ... like footfalls on carpet ... yet not human ... longer ... loping – like a dog – and as the realisation came to her, there it was, its wet nose pressed against the glass, its pink tongue lolling, its floppy jaws slobbering. About one golden eye was a circle of black.

'Patch?' Janet called. 'Are you Patch?' Once, twice, three times it raised a paw and planted it against the glass. Janet saw the pink and velvety pads, the fluting of its claws. 'You're just a puppy,' she said. 'Who taught you to shake hands? Lola? Is Lola there? Is she?'

She reached out to place her own hand flat against the glass to match the offered paw. At once the dog sprang up on its hind legs, its front paws reaching the third panel of glass, its smooth pink belly fully exposed, its long thin tail whipping from side to side. 'You're a girl too,' she said, noticing. 'So I shouldn't be scared of you, should I?'

As if in answer, the animal suddenly dropped down, bolted to the door, and thrust its nose under, pawing at the edge of the concrete floor, whining.

'All right,' she said. 'All right. I'm coming.' She pushed herself up and the book fell to the floor, forgotten. Grasping her bag, she opened the door and stepped out.

There was nothing. No dog. No Lola. Only darkness. 'Lola?' she called. 'Lola?' Nothing. 'Patch? Patchy?' She bent and whistled low. Suddenly the animal bounded towards her from the direction of the bridge, and rolled on its back at her feet, offering its stomach to be patted. 'You are disgusting,' she said, dropping to her knees and stroking it. 'You are totally without shame.'

But when the dog leapt up again and launched into a series of play-bows intended to lure her into further games, Janet stepped back and looked about. Nowhere was there a sign of Lola. Janet put her hands on her hips and shook her head in mock reprimand. 'So,' she said, 'where is your mistress ... hmmmm?'

At once the animal began a series of low growls and, raising its haunches, dragged its front legs backwards in the dirt.

'What?' she said. 'What is it?'

Again the growling was repeated – not threatening, but insistent – this time accompanied by a turning of the head, until Janet leaned down, curious. 'Are you telling me something? Is that it? Lola? Is it Lola?'

As if in answer, the dog leapt away, bounded back, then leapt away again, its head nodding, its tail beating from side to side.

'Where is she? Patch, where's Lola? Show me. Where's Lola?'

This time there could be no doubt. The dog turned away completely, taking three or four leaps towards the bridge, then waited, its tail wagging, until Janet had begun to follow.

'Go on,' she said, waving it forward with both hands. 'Go on. Where is she? Where's Lola? Show me, go on.'

The animal crossed the clearing in the direction of the bridge, stopping to wait at the edge of the scrubby incline that led down to the gully. Running, Janet caught up to it. 'Down there?' she said, her throat constricting. 'Lola is down there?' The dog vanished momentarily into the thick, dank grasses, only to emerge, barking furiously. 'Wait!' she called, pushing her way into the undergrowth. 'Just wait!'

Again the animal bolted away, down a path that followed the contours of the bank. Like a cattle path worn into the bank by some animal, Janet thought, stumbling along behind. She tried to keep sight of the dog's tail without losing her footing, but the path fell very steeply and she stopped, looking up to check her whereabouts. Not 20 metres from her was the bridge and, beneath it, awful darkness.

'Patch,' she called. 'Patchy, stop. Stop, please.' She raised her hands to her mouth, and, cupping them, called, 'Lola? Lola? Are you there?'

Nothing.

She went on a few paces, wary of the steepness of the bank, the possibility of falling. She stopped and called again.

'Lola! If you're there, answer me! Answer me or come out! I hate this game. Lola!'

Nothing.

The animal did not stop. Each time she called, it returned to her, skipping and turning upon itself, determined to lead her on. So she followed. She caught herself on roots, falling to bark her shins; she brushed against a patch of nettles, feeling their searing burn, but she did not stop. She could not. If this was not a game, if Lola was there beneath the bridge, in trouble, in the darkness ... If Lola was a friend ...

When she reached the bridge she stood still, her hands again at her face. Must she go on? Must she go beneath, into that darkness, into that awful belly of darkness?

. She searched for courage. She whispered, 'Lola? Lola?' hoping to hear, longing to hear; and

softly, from beneath the bridge, she heard, 'Janet ...
Janet ...' no more than a whisper, the faintest exhalation of breath. She was certain of it. She was certain that she heard.

She peered into the dark.

At first she could make out nothing. Then, by the silver bands falling from the gaps in the planking above, she thought she saw Patch – or Patch's eyes, twin glimmers of gold – high up in the furthest, darkest space, where the bank met the timbers of the bearers. And there was a smell. A musty animal smell.

'Patch?' she said, then, 'Lola?'

As she spoke the eyes vanished, and appeared again, higher, almost above her.

'Lola?' she pleaded.

Nothing.

She drew in her breath. 'Lola, I'm sick of this. If this is a game I hate it. Come out. Come out now.'

The eyes narrowed, cruel and sneering.

'Lola. If you don't come out now you're not my friend. You're like the rest. Tricking me. If you are I couldn't care. I was all right by myself. I don't need you. And anyway, I lost your stupid troll ...'

Before her, out of the darkness, the white dog appeared. It reared on its hind legs, standing tall, as tall as herself, then pranced, pawing in the darkness, stretching, growing, its form constantly altering, taking new shape before Janet's face. Human shape. White, fleshy. Yet there, circling one eye, was the mark of the dog; the black patch.

'Patch?'

Janet's lips could hardly move.

'Lola?'

At the sound of the name the eyes flickered and the patch grew fluid, spreading, covering the white flesh all over with hair, blue-black and lustrous, stinking of damp, musty.

And suddenly, as in the clearest dream, Janet knew what loomed before her. Neither dog nor human. But a beast, a shambling blue-black beast.

She cried out, forcing her swollen tongue, her stubborn lips to make one final plea. And as the talons of the thing came down upon her, tearing her, and its arms or chest or mouth enveloped her, a word freed itself from the darkness and rang throughout the clearing, rising and falling to fade and die far away in the dismal bush: 'Friend,' it echoed, 'friend.'

When the last bus clattered over the bridge and pulled into the terminus, the driver leaned down to check that the clearing was empty. He would have been very surprised if it was not; in all his years on the midnight run, he had never collected a soul from the Bent-Back Bridge terminus. He had set down a few, but never ... yet there, on the ground outside the phone box, was a bag. A duffel bag.

He opened the door of the bus and clambered out. He crossed the clearing and stood, looking about. No one. He reached down and picked the bag up. It had been ripped wide open. From the phone box came a fluttering sound. There was a book, its pages turning this way and that. He

46

opened the door and lifted the book by its pages. He looked about again.

Nobody.

He put the book in the bag. But as he turned to go, a sudden movement caught his eye. Something quick and furtive. It came again. He stood still, watching, and from the darkness behind the phone box there appeared a dog: white, with a blue-black patch about one golden eye.

'Hello, Patchy,' he said as the animal rolled at his feet. 'Are you hanging around again? I haven't seen you for a while. Don't you have a home to go to? You had me worried for a minute,' and as he stooped to pat its stomach, there, in the dirt, he saw something bright. He picked it up and turned it in his fingers: a sort of horror doll, a troll thing with a silver chain dangling from its head of blue-black hair. 'The things kids play with,' he muttered, then he turned and tossed it away, far over the clearing.

But the dog saw and sprang up, bounding after it into the deepest darkness beneath the Bent-Back Bridge.